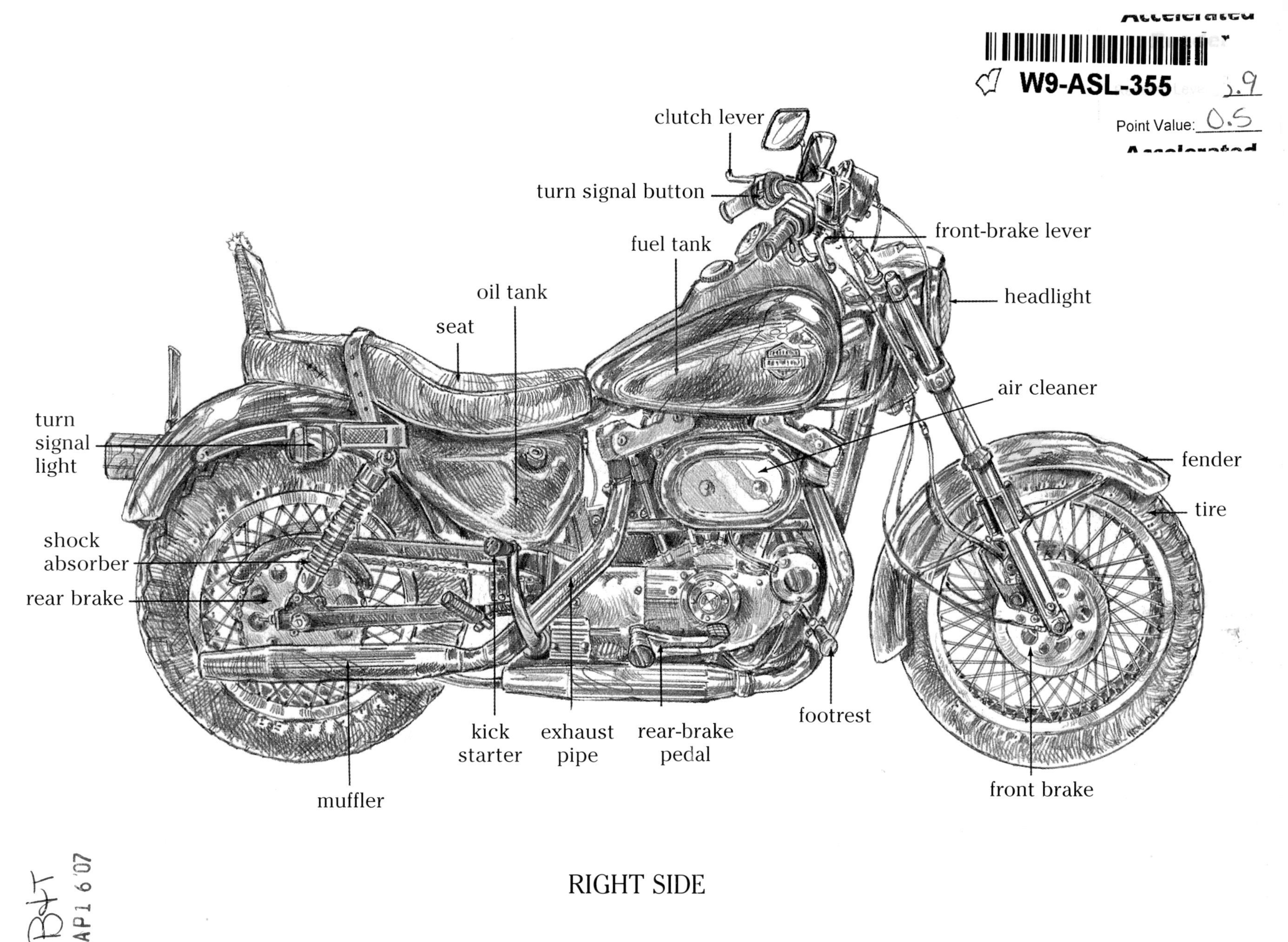
clutch lever
turn signal button
front-brake lever
fuel tank
oil tank
headlight
seat
air cleaner
turn
signal
light
fender
tire
shock
absorber
rear brake
kick
starter
exhaust
pipe
rear-brake
pedal
footrest
muffler
front brake

RIGHT SIDE

BEVERLY CLEARY

Lucky Chuck

ILLUSTRATED BY J. WINSLOW HIGGINBOTTOM

HarperCollins*Publishers*

The author and illustrator wish to thank Dennis Rietwyk and Ellen DeMilto of Harley Davidson of New York City, Inc., for their assistance in the preparation of this book.

Lucky Chuck
 • www.harperchildrens.com

Library of Congress Cataloging-in-Publication Data • Cleary, Beverly.
Lucky Chuck. • Summary: A young boy who throws caution and the Motor Vehicle Code to the wind during a reckless motorcycle ride is brought to his senses by a Highway Patrol officer.
[1. Motorcycling—Fiction] I. Higginbottom, J. Winslow, ill. II. Title.
PZ7.C5792Luc 1984 [E] 83-13386
ISBN 0-688-02736-9 • ISBN 0-06-008239-9 (pbk.)

Typography by Jeanne Hogle
1 2 3 4 5 6 7 8 9 10
❖

This is Chuck. He pumps gas after school.

This is Chuck's motorcycle. "My bike," he calls it.
Chuck is proud of his bike. He bought it secondhand.
A few dents and scratches don't bother Chuck.

This is Chuck's motorcycle-driver's license. He earned it by studying the Motor Vehicle Code and passing a driver's test.

This is Chuck's mother worrying about Chuck and his motorcycle.

This is Chuck dressed to ride his motorcycle. He is wearing a safety helmet with a shatterproof face shield, a sturdy light-colored jacket with a zipper, rugged pants, leather gloves with cuffs, and heavy boots. Chuck feels big and important.

This is Chuck checking his gas tank
after he mounts his motorcycle.
He has plenty of gas.

This is the off-on switch Chuck flips
to the run position, after he opens
the gas valve and turns the key.

This is the choke he pulls
that helps start the engine.

This is Chuck's right foot kicking the kick starter.
Cha-kung.

This is the headlight Chuck turns on. The Motor Vehicle Code says he must, even in the daytime.

This is Chuck's left hand pulling in the clutch lever that disengages the engine.

This is Chuck's left foot moving the peg that puts his bike into first gear. *Vroom-vroom! Ratta-tatta, ratta-tatta.*

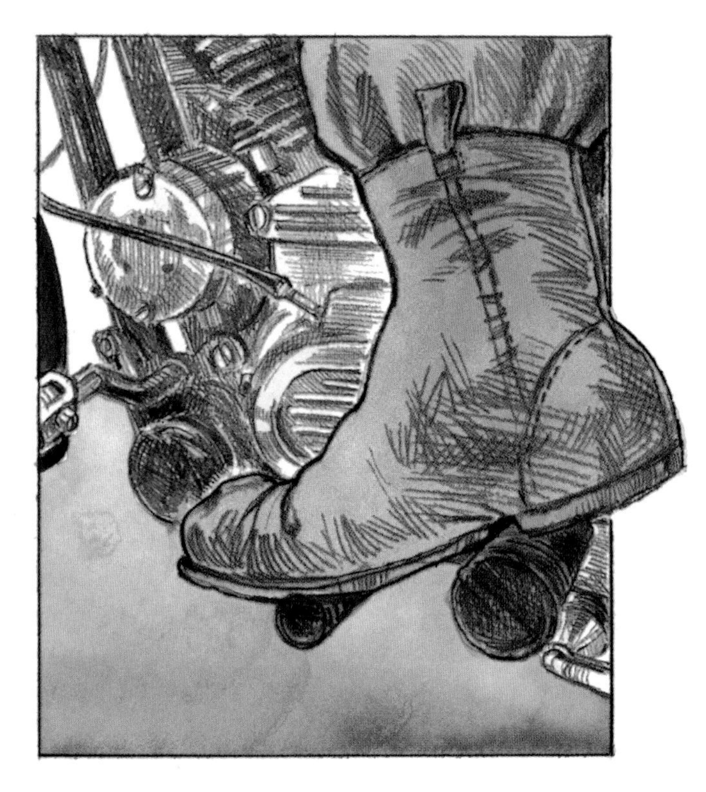

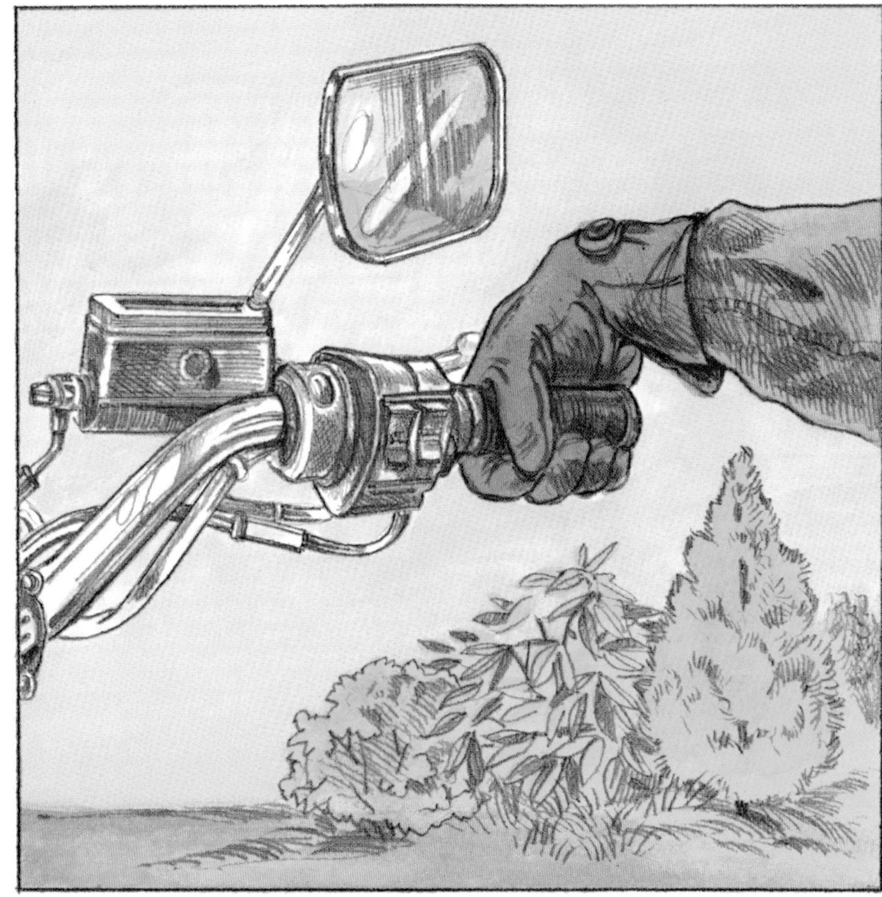

This is Chuck's right hand turning the throttle that gives his engine the gas.

Chuck's left hand lets out the clutch. Now he's moving. Beautiful!

This is Chuck's mother shouting, "Be careful, Chuck! Don't lay it down," as he shifts to second gear and rides away. Chuck's mother has heard so much motorcycle talk from Chuck that she knows bikers don't fall over, they "lay it down."

This is Chuck flashing his turn signal before he leans his motorcycle and rounds the corner—just like riding a bicycle, only better. So far so good.

This is a mean dog chasing Chuck. *Grrrr-grrrr.* Chuck remembers the Motor Vehicle Code says he should never kick a dog because he might lose control of his motorcycle and lay it down.

When the dog is close, he upshifts
to second gear . . .

and speeds away. Good-bye, dog.

This is the speedometer, which tells Chuck how fast he is going . . .

and this is the tachometer, which tells Chuck how many times a minute his engine turns over. When the needle on the tachometer approaches the red line, Chuck must shift to the next gear or ruin his engine. Quick, Chuck! Shift to third gear!

Wow! There are trees and telephone poles flying past Chuck. *Whish, whish, whish.*

Spit! Spat! These are bugs splattering Chuck's face shield.

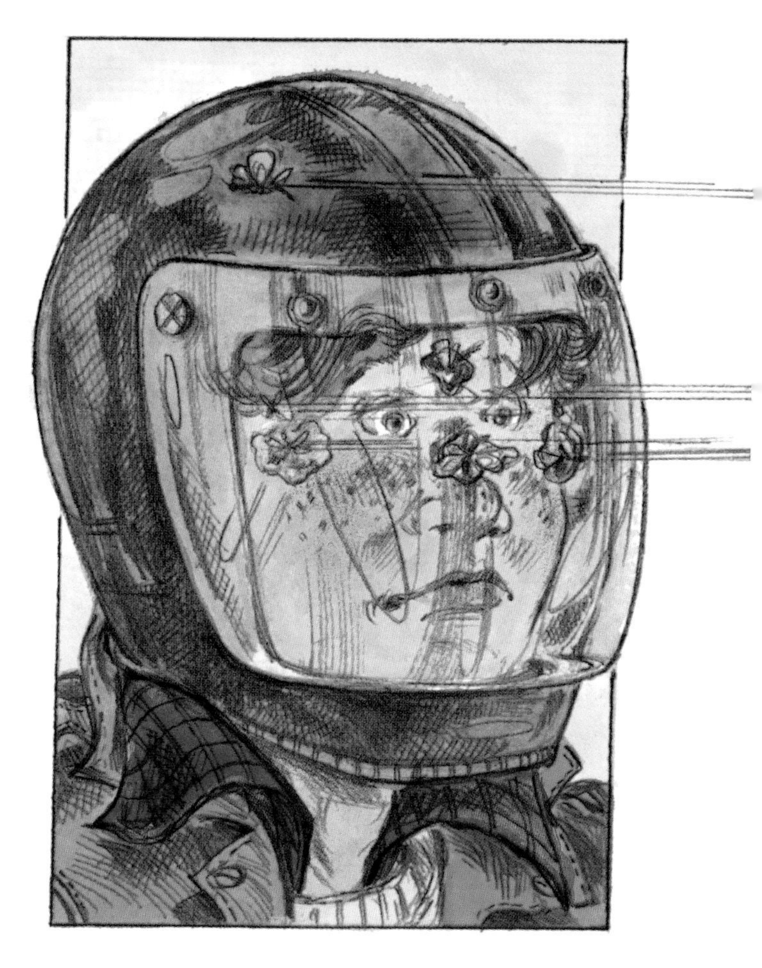

Chuck goes faster, weaving in and out of traffic. *Toot-toot! Honk-honk!* Drivers are mad at Chuck. "Crazy kid!" they yell. "You want to get killed?"

Now Chuck is riding down the white line in the center of the pavement. He is having such a good time he forgets the Motor Vehicle Code. What does it know about fun?

WESTSIDE
MOVERS

This is Chuck passing a truck—*BEEP! BEEP! BEEP!*—that makes such a draft it nearly blows his motorcycle off the road. Whew! That was close. Lucky Chuck.

This is Chuck after he shifts to fourth gear to stay ahead of the truck. Wow-ee! Chuck is really moving.

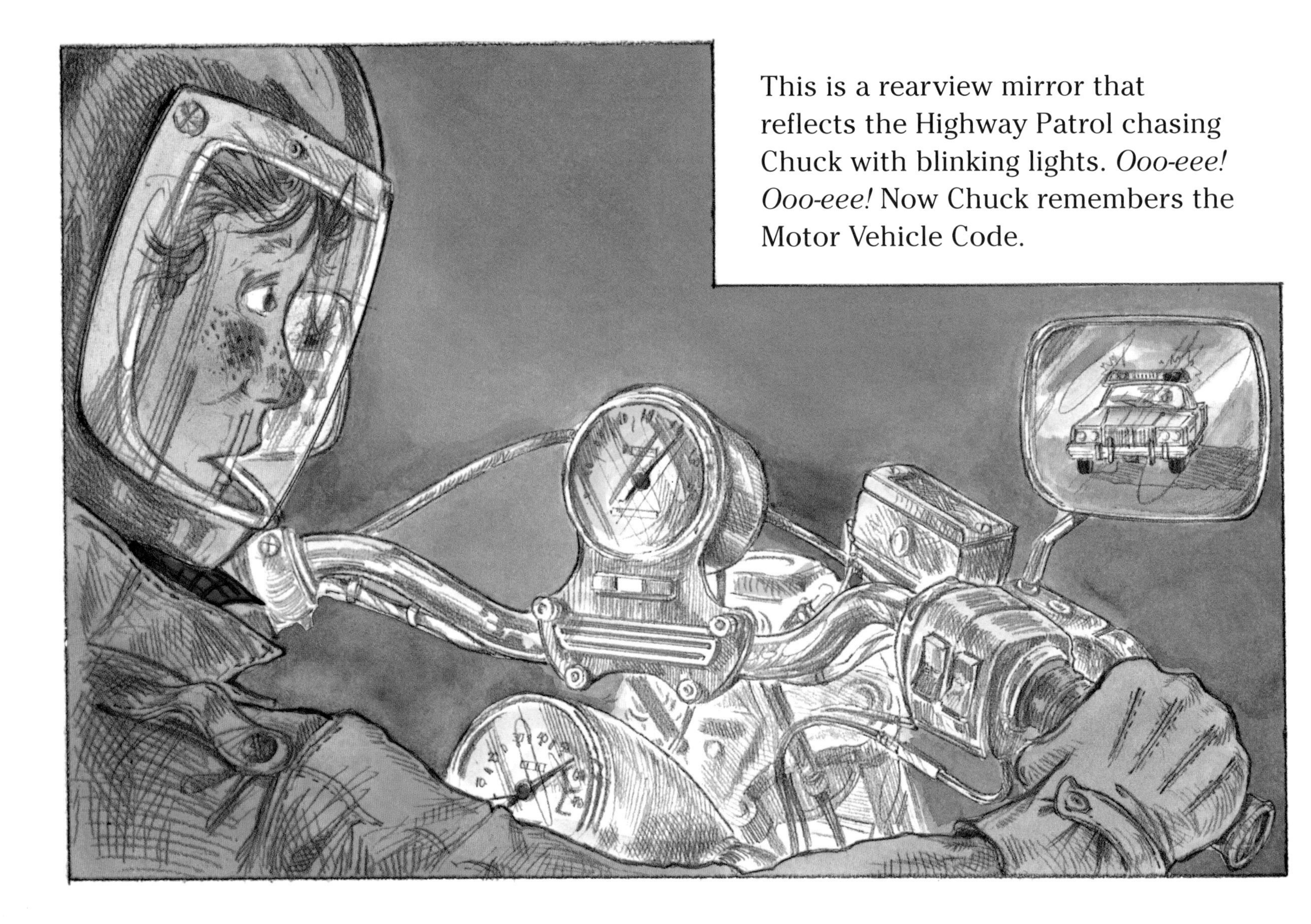

This is a rearview mirror that reflects the Highway Patrol chasing Chuck with blinking lights. *Ooo-eee! Ooo-eee! Ooo-eee!* Now Chuck remembers the Motor Vehicle Code.

This is Chuck applying the front brake with his hand and the rear brake with his foot. He makes a mistake and steps too hard on the rear brake.

This is scared Chuck riding with his back wheel locked and skidding back and forth on the pavement. Fishtailing, bikers call it.

This is Chuck trying to downshift through all the gears as the patrol car gains on him. He does not see a patch of gravel on the pavement.

This is unlucky Chuck skidding on the gravel and laying it down. *Thump! Bump!* Chuck flies off his bike into some weeds. Yow! Ouch!

Sparks fly as the motorcycle slides on the pavement.
The patrol car pulls up behind Chuck.

This is Chuck struggling to lift his motorcycle, which he leans on its side stand as the officer climbs out of his patrol car.

This is the officer writing Chuck a ticket for speeding and reckless driving. Chuck hurts all over.

This is Chuck kicking the edge of the pavement while the officer lectures him on the dangers of daredevil driving.

People in passing cars slow down to stare at Chuck, who is embarrassed and ashamed. The officer tells Chuck he is lucky to be alive.

This is Chuck wearing his helmet again as he rides home. He sits straight, with his arms slightly bent. He follows at a safe distance behind the left wheel of the car in front so the driver can see him in the rearview mirror. He watches the road for holes, bumps, gravel, and wet leaves. Whoever wrote the Motor Vehicle Code would be proud of Chuck.

This is Chuck passing the mean dog, who knows he can't catch Chuck.

This is Chuck arriving safely home. "See, Mom," he says, "nothing to worry about."

This is Chuck with aching bones, thinking about the wisdom of the Motor Vehicle Code and how much gas he will have to pump to pay his traffic fine.

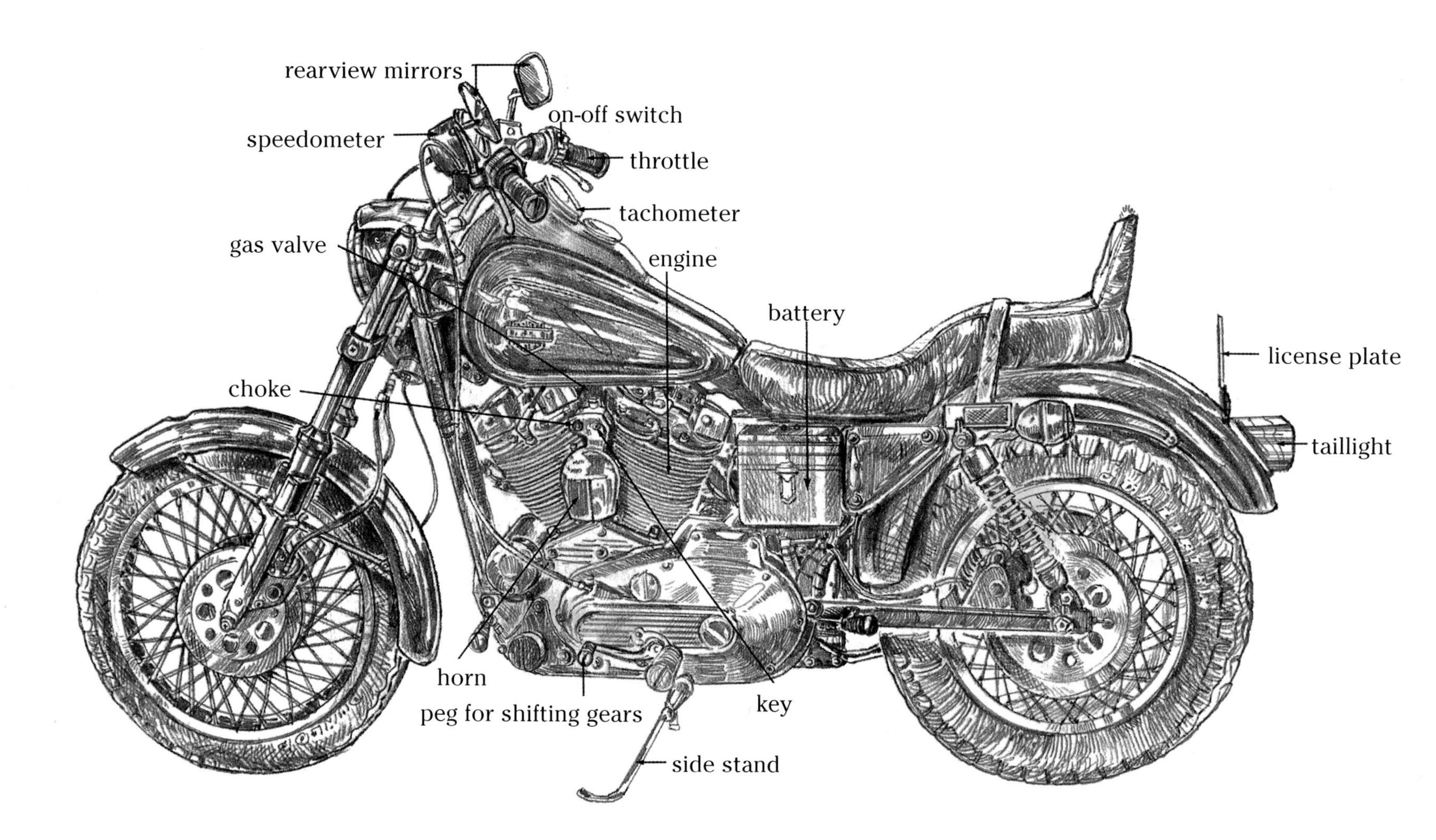
rearview mirrors
on-off switch
speedometer
throttle
tachometer
gas valve
engine
battery
license plate
choke
taillight
horn
key
peg for shifting gears
side stand

LEFT SIDE